D0607545

For Millie and Poppy with love – GM

First American edition published in 2000 by Carolrhoda Books, Inc.

Designed by Ian Butterworth

Published by arrangement with Transworld Publishers, London, England,
a division of the Random House Group Ltd.

Carolrhoda Books, Inc., a division of Lerner Publishing Group
241 First Avenue North, Minneapolis, MN 55401 U.S.A.

Website address: www.lernerbooks.com

Library of Congress Cataloging-in-Publication Data
McCaughrean, Geraldine.
Beauty and the beast / by Geraldine McCaughrean ; illustrated
by Gary Blythe.
p. c.m.
Summary: Through her great capacity to love, a kind and beautiful maid releases a handsome prince from the spell which has made him into an ugly beast.
ISBN 1-57505-491-4 (lib. bdg.: alk. paper)
[1. Fairy tales. 2. Folklore—France.] I. Blythe, Gary, ill. II. Title.
PZ8.M1718 Be 2000
398.2'044'02—dc21 00-008023

Printed in Belgium

1 2 3 4 5 6 - 05 04 03 02 01 00

BEAUTY AND THE BEAST

GERALDINE McCAUGHREAN

Illustrated by GARY BLYTHE

Carolrhoda Books, Inc., Minneapolis

Into a forest of fifty thousand trees rode a lone traveler. Overhead, the moon was a smoking mirror. When it disappeared behind a monstrous paw of cloud, so did Gregor's path, and he was utterly lost.

The leaves brushed his face like the fingers of ghosts. The twigs clawed his cloak. Under him his horse trembled with terror.

"Steady now, boy. There's a light up ahead," said Gregor, "and you know what that means — a warm fire and a friendly face."

But the light was not a cottage window, only the moon glinting on a piece of broken glass — no, a fragment of mirror.

Strangely, as Gregor leaned over it, the reflection was not of treetops and stars, but of towers, chandeliers, and silverware. And when he looked up, he was not out-of-doors at all, but inside a sumptuous palace.

"Hello? Is anybody there?"

No one came. Only his own shadow, thrown by a log fire, danced across the painted ceiling. And yet there must be someone in the house. Who had lit the fire? Who had laid the table with hot bread, cold meat, and mulled wine? Gregor sat down and ate.

Who had piled the feather pillows six-deep on the bed in the great, white bedroom? Gregor lay down and slept, while outside rain beat down.

The next morning he walked through the palace, looking for its owner at first, then just looking in breathless amazement. Every corridor was lined with great gilded mirrors, each one cracked like broken ice. Every vase was filled with fresh flowers, every statue blindfolded with a scarf of silk.

"My daughter Lotte would give her soul for those," thought Gregor as he saw the diamonds strung into chandeliers.

"My daughter Gitta would give her soul for those," he thought as he passed racks of white fur capes and rows of satin shoes.

"Oh, my daughter Beauty would love these!" he thought as he came to a courtyard overrun with roses. And thinking it could do no harm, he picked one bloom to take home.

Ungrateful villain! You have plundered my house! Now pay the price!" rasped a voice. "Tell me one reason that I should not eat you, flesh and bone!"

"No, no! Don't kill me! I'll give you anything, but let me live! I'm a rich man. I'll give you ships, cargoes, spices —" but Gregor's voice broke. For suddenly a beast filled the doorway — a walking nightmare so hideous that Gregor thought he would die of looking.

"I picked the rose for my daughter Beauty. I meant no harm!" Gregor sobbed, falling to his knees.

"Then swear to pay the price!"

Gregor swore an oath as deep as the sea: "Whatever you ask, I'll pay it."

"Then bring me the daughter for whom you picked the rose. Bring me Beauty! *She* is the price!"

Gregor reached out two hands as if to grab back his promise. "Not Beauty! Take me, not Beauty!" But the Beast had gone. So too had his palace, and Gregor knelt alone on the forest floor.

Gregor's horse carried him home at a gallop. Waiting at the door stood his three daughters.

"What have you brought me?" asked Lotte.

"More than last time, I hope," said Gitta.

But Beauty kissed him on the cheek and brought him tea and took his coat and hat. "Welcome home. Oh, you brought me a rose, Papa! Thank you!"

How could he tell her? How could he say, "That rose has cost you your life?"

"Forget your promise," said Lotte when Gregor told his story.

"Send her abroad," said Gitta. "Somewhere the Beast can't reach her."

But Beauty said, "I will go, Father. A promise given must be a promise kept."

A horse came to the door next day, drooping its reins on the step. Beauty climbed into the saddle and said, "Take me where I must go."

The horse took her over fields and fells, down lanes and through forests, until its hoof struck a piece of broken mirror, and Beauty found herself in the palace of the Beast.

No one greeted her but her own shadow dancing on the wall. No one waited on her, and yet the table was set and the fire lit and the bed warmed for her to sleep in. Beauty lay down, trembling, every moment waiting for teeth to sink into her, for claws to tear her. The firelight died to a glow, and at last she could bear the fear no longer:

"Kill me, Beast, if you are going to!" she called into the menacing dark. "Waiting is worse than dying!" There was no reply.

As night turned to morning and winter turned to spring, Beauty waited, but the Beast still did not eat her. He did not even show himself, but he left her to wander the great house alone, fingering the sculptures, smelling the roses. "What do you want of me?" she called out to the footsteps that echoed behind her on the lightless stairs.

There was no reply.

Every morning she found little presents on the end of her bed — a dress, playing cards, a book. Every mealtime there were fresh flowers on the table, a glass of wine poured, and an empty seat opposite hers. She ate and played and walked . . . alone, except for the occasional sound of breathing nearby. Loneliness smothered her like an eiderdown.

At last, she hardly cared how ugly the unseen Beast might be. So she waited on the stairs in the dark, silent and still, and reached out a hand as he went by.

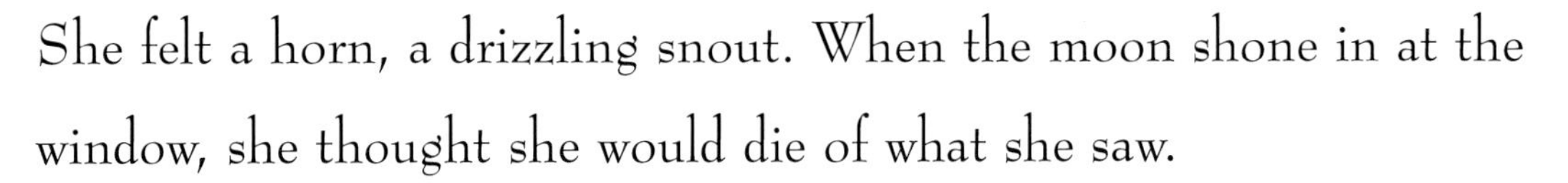

She felt a horn, a drizzling snout. When the moon shone in at the window, she thought she would die of what she saw.

But she did not die. And she did not run away, because she was promised to the Beast, and nothing is as vile as a broken promise.

"Well? Am I not the ugliest sight you ever saw?"

"I have seen very little of the world," said Beauty, because it was not in her nature to say an unkind thing.

Beast owned a magic mirror, one through which he saw the outside world without ever leaving the echoing silence of his palace. In it, just by wishing, Beauty could see her family and friends and far more besides. It showed her many things she had never seen before.

The next day, sitting on the stairs, silent and still, Beauty waited for the Beast to pass by. Then she reached out a hand. "Eat with me tonight, Beast. Please."

hey dined by candlelight.

"Well? Am I not the vilest sight you ever saw?" asked Beast.

"No, I saw a war in your magic looking glass. That was far worse," Beauty replied.

"Does my face not disgust you?"

"No, I saw famine in your magic glass. That disgusted me."

"Does the sight of me not put you off your food?" muttered Beast.

"Nothing puts me off my food!" said Beauty, and she laughed — which was strange for the Beast, because he had not heard laughter for a hundred years.

"I suppose you hate me for holding you captive here."

"I don't hate anyone," said Beauty.

"And that is why you are called Beauty," said Beast. There were tears in the hollows of his eyes.

They dined together always after that. They walked though the rose gardens and between the broken mirrors. They talked about books and gardens and music, and they played chess. Beauty no longer noticed his ugliness. Beast, though, took her beauty to heart more every day. It seemed to fill him with despair.

Beauty missed her home. In the magic glass she saw her father staring into the fire or slumped in his chair, unkempt and wild-eyed, blaming himself for his bargain with the Beast.

"Let me visit my family," she said.

"NEVER!"

"I would come back, I swear it."

But Beast stamped his hoof and snatched hold of her arm, her hair, her dress. He clung on, like a man on the brink of a precipice.

It took her a week to persuade him. On the day she left, frost settled on the garden, black like soot.

"Take my magic glass," he told her. "When you are in the outside world, it will show you this one. My world."

"I'll be back before you even miss me," she said blithely.

"I miss you already," he complained, thrusting a rose at her.

But as she rode, the rose turned brittle and broke, so that she arrived home empty-handed.

Her father's face was wonderful to see. He laughed and cried, cheered and sang. "Did the Beast spare you? God bless him! God bless him!"

"Did you bring me a present?" asked Gitta, staring.

"Did you bring me any of his jewels?" asked Lotte, scrabbling in the saddlebag. "Oh, fooh! Nothing but a stupid tin mirror!"

Beauty would have stayed only a day or two. But Gitta was to be married, so she stayed for the wedding. Lotte's birthday was coming, so Beauty stayed for that too. Days gave way to weeks, and never once did she think to look in the magic mirror, though she told herself often: I shall go back. Soon.

The room was pitch dark, but under Beauty's pillow the little mirror held a star-bright nebula of whirling dreams. They dazzled her with moonlit pictures. There was the sour green lawn pitching like the deck of a ship. There was the towering clock, reaching out to her with pleading hands. There were the stable doors swinging.

In the rose garden, the last scarlet petals of the last rose fell like drops of blood, splashing, splashing, splashing onto the face of . . .

"BEAST!"

Beauty woke, the room full of her own screaming.

"Beast! Beast! Don't die! *I'm coming! Wait for me!"*

orget Father's promise," said Lotte. "Don't go back."

But Beauty only fumbled with the bridle and clambered onto the magic horse's back.

"Don't go!" called Gregor, but Beauty's eyes saw nothing but the rosebushes, their twigs dripping black tar. Her ears rang with that terrible cry.

"*Beast is dying!*" she shouted over her shoulder. "*I must go to him!*"

Faster than the pounce of wolves or snow falling from a roof, the magic horse carried Beauty back to the palace. She ran through the great hall, past the fire dead in its grate, over shards of mirror fallen from the gilded frames. She threw open the wrought-gold gate to the garden, and she slithered over tar to where Beast lay on his face, frost-blackened, still as death.

She caught up his great head, and whole handfuls of fur came away in her hands. Her tears crawled into his shaggy ears as she howled: "Oh Beast, I'm sorry! I betrayed you. I broke my promise. Oh Beast, my lovely Beast! Why didn't you kill me when I first came? Better to be dead than to see you die!"

Arched over him, like a beast over its prey, she kissed his chilly face. "I loved you, Beast. I loved you!"

Like the petals falling from roses, the pelt fell from the Beast's back and caught on the tarry thorns.

Beauty sprang back in alarm, for between her hands she found a young man's head. "Who are you? What have you done with my Beast?"

"Don't you recognize me?" said the young man. "Don't you know me? I am Beast. I was Beast. For a hundred years, I wore the curse of Beast."

Even his voice was different — musical and mild. She narrowed her eyes at him, touched his curly hair. Warily she circled him, looking him up and down. "Is it you? Is it really you?"

"As a prince I was vain and spoiled," he explained. "I broke the hearts of those who loved me. An enchantress cursed me for my beastliness. 'Be cursed,' she said, 'until someone loves you for yourself alone!'. . . And you saw the curse she laid on me."

Around them, the palace began to melt like winter ice. The turrets put on green branches. The stained glass changed to birds, the marble stairs to grass slopes, the ceilings to canopies of leaves. "Now we can begin again," said the Prince. "Somewhere new."

"So long as our love can stay the same," said Beauty, plucking a tuft of fur from the thorns of a wild rose.

But she need not have feared. Underneath his noble bearing and pleasant face was the same old Beast to whom Beauty had given her heart.

And though they both changed with time, as people will, the love between them only grew sweeter and more beautiful over the years.

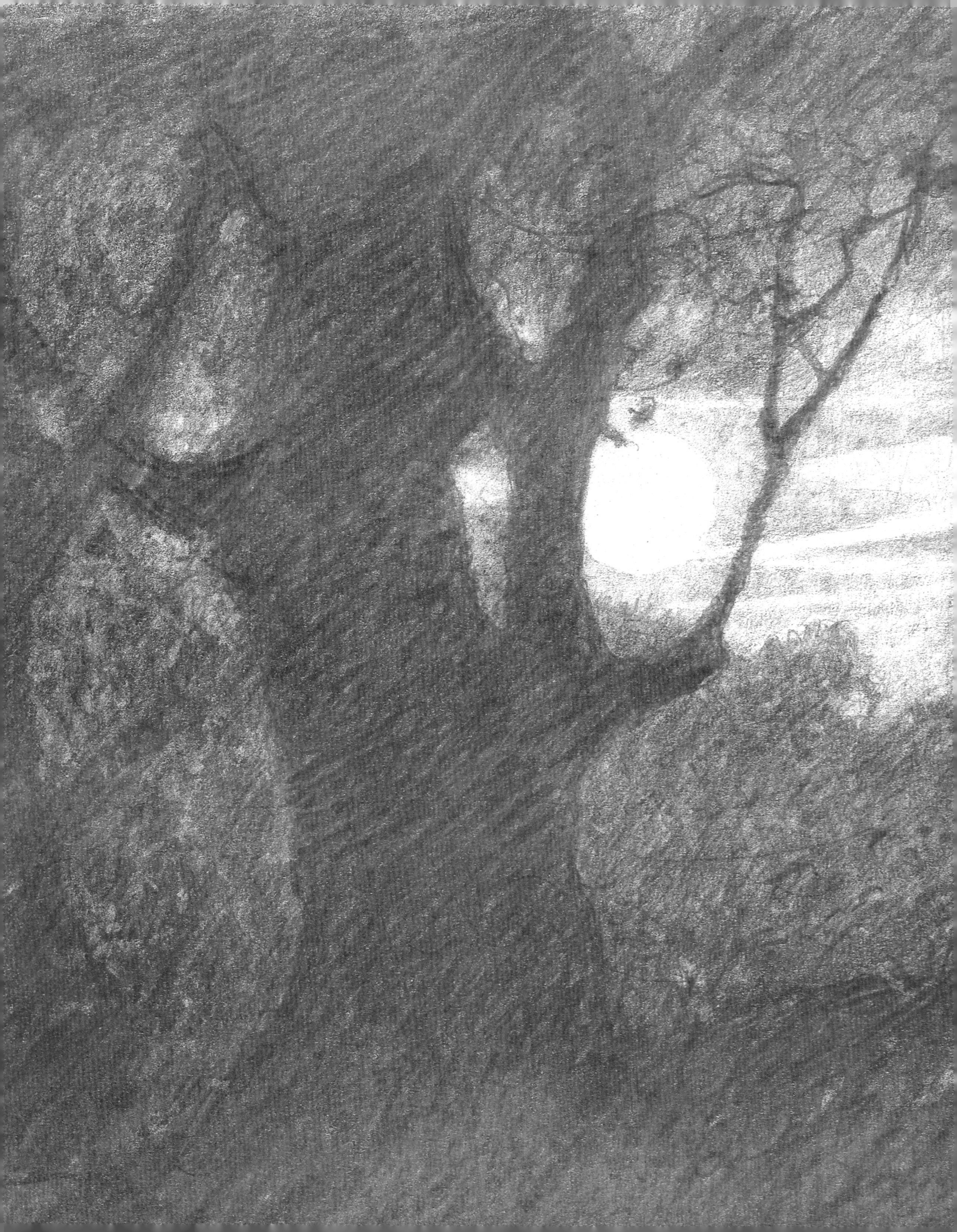